Printed in the United States of America First Printing, 2017

ISBN 978-0-692-89846-8
Written by Ryan Avery
Cover design by Carole Roemer
Illustrations by Carole Roemer
Edits by Serena Fisher
Formatting by Jon Firman
AveryToday, Inc.
PO BOX 1516
Englewood, CO 80150

100% of the profits from this book are shared with non-profit organizations that educate and empower girls and young women.

Share your story and connect with girls all around the world with
#YesOhYesSheDid

To my daughter Atlas,

you are my world!

There once lived a girl

In a BIG
round world

Who was told what to do.

Sweep, mop, cook! And always remember to vacuum! Don't think about dreaming, being or believing in the things you want to do. For you are here to support others – but not yourself – and that's what you should want to do.

But the girl wanted more.
She wanted to build and fly. She wanted to write and work.
She wanted to dream and travel, to own businesses
and wear more than skirts.

She wanted to run, and play, get dirty and say, "I am going to be somebody someday!" And so she started. But it was harder than she thought! Some people didn't help her. Some people didn't like her. And nearly every one of them said she should stop. They told her, "Good girls like you need to move out of the way and be silent so others can do."

She didn't like what some of them said.
So she said... NO!

She declared, "I will not sit back.
It's my turn to learn and I will!
I will; watch me I will.
I will fight back!"
So she did!

They said she shouldn't learn about math, science and art.
But, she didn't listen and decided,
"I will learn about math, science and art."
And guess what? She did!

ATLAS, INC.

They said she should
work for someone else
because that's what you are
supposed to do!

But she wanted to build
her own business because
that's what she wanted to do!

So guess what? She did!

She wanted to write and blog and share her words with the world!
Many people told her she couldn't. "You're too young!" they said.
"You have nothing to say!" they told her. "Be quiet! they yelled. And guess what?
She didn't listen to them, and she started writing and blogging.
Oh yes, oh yes, oh yes she did!

They warned, "Stay put and don't travel much. It's dangerous out there, so don't think about it too much!" But she wanted to travel and taste. She wanted to see and get out of this place! And guess what? She did! She found friends that supported her, and she learned more than she thought. She had an absolute blast! She even realized that you can do anything – as hard as it might be – as long as you get started and always believe.

"No this, no that," they all said. "Don't do this, don't do that!" they screamed.
"It's not what a good girl like you should do, so we beg you to sit back and relax
please, please!" But the girl had different plans. She had many, many dreams.
"I want to do everything I can while I am here," she said,
"that's my plan and I will, I will, I will." And guess what? She did!

She traveled, wrote, and dreamed.
She laughed and believed and even wore jeans.
She had fun and adventure, started businesses, even found
her Mister Right!

One day, when everyone realized she could do anything, they all asked for her advice. And she did what none of them had ever done. She encouraged them to go after their dreams. She told everyone, "Good for you!"

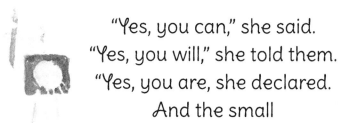

"Yes, you can," she said.
"Yes, you will," she told them.
"Yes, you are, she declared.
And the small

little girl who grew
up in that big round world
changed the path for
all who followed.
And guess what? Follow they did!

Oh yes, oh Yes, oh yes, oh yes, oh yes, oh yes she did!

PS – Going back to that "Mr. Right" part... `
Together the boy and girl lived in a loving partnership
happily ever after.
They worked to help all
the boys and girls around
the world accomplish
their big BIG dreams.

Oh yes, oh yes, oh yes,
oh yes, oh yes,
oh yes THEY did!

DREAM BIG!

CPSIA information can be obtained
at www.ICGtesting.com
Printed in the USA
LVOW05*1518140917
548741LV00025B/369/P